SHADOWS OF DESIRE

E.B. FOX

CHAPTER 1

The club pulses with a dark heartbeat as I step inside, my emerald dress shimmering under the low lights. Smoke curls around writhing bodies, their faces masks of ecstasy and despair. I scan the crowd for Jenna's familiar laugh—she's why I'm here after all—but my gaze snags on a figure lurking in the shadows, and I pause.

A man, tall and imposing, his eyes piercing through the gloom to lock onto mine. A shiver runs down my spine. I don't know what it is about him, but I can't look away.

My heart races. His presence draws me in like a moth to flame. I drift closer, weaving through the throng of revelers. The air grows thick, charged with unspoken sin.

A hand on my arm. I turn, startled.

"Alana," Jenna squeals, "you made it!" Her words fade to a dull roar as I search for the mysterious stranger. Gone. Vanished like a phantom.

I paste on a smile. "Happy birthday," I say, but my mind drifts to piercing blue eyes and danger.

The night wears on. Drinks flow. Laughter echoes. Yet I feel hollow, searching every dark corner.

Then *he's* there, materializing at my side like smoke given form.

"You look lost," he murmurs, voice like velvet and broken glass. "Can I offer you a drink?"

My heart pounds. "I don't know you," I say, voice steadier than I feel.

A ghost of a smile. "Marcus Blackwood. And you're Alana Carter, the advertising wunderkind."

Surprise flickers across my face. "You've done your homework."

"I make it my business to know interesting people." He signals the bartender. "Gin and tonic for the lady. Neat whiskey for me."

I arch an eyebrow. "Presumptuous."

"Am I wrong?"

The drinks arrive. I take a sip, the gin sharp on my tongue. "Lucky guess."

His eyes gleam with amusement and something darker. "I don't believe in luck."

"What do you believe in, Mr. Blackwood?"

"Please, call me Marcus." He leans closer, his breath warm on my ear. "I believe in seizing opportunities when they present themselves."

A thrill runs through me, equal parts excitement and warning. I should walk away. Instead, I find myself drawn deeper into his orbit.

"And what opportunity are you seizing tonight?" I ask, voice low.

His smile is a knife's edge. "That remains to be seen."

I lean in, drawn by his magnetic pull. "And what lies beneath that carefully crafted exterior, Marcus?"

His eyes darken, a storm brewing. "Demons you're better off not knowing, Alana."

A chill races down my spine, but I can't look away. "We all have our shadows," I whisper.

"Some darker than others." His fingers brush mine, electricity sparking. "What haunts you in the quiet hours?"

Images flash—coastal cliffs, shattered dreams, a life unlived. I swallow hard. "Regrets. The roads not taken."

"Ah," he nods, understanding in his eyes. "The siren call of the unknown."

"And you?" I press, heart racing. "What keeps Marcus Blackwood awake at night?"

His jaw tightens. "The price of power. The weight of choices that can't be unmade."

The air between us grows heavy, charged. I should feel afraid, but instead, I'm intoxicated.

Marcus's gaze turns razor-sharp. "You should stay away from me, Alana. I'm not a good man."

"I'm not looking for a good man," I breathe, surprising myself.

He grips my wrist, gentle but firm. "You don't know what you're asking for."

"Then show me," I challenge, pulse thrumming beneath his touch.

Marcus's eyes flash with hunger and something like pain. "Be careful what you wish for," he warns, voice rough. "There's no going back."

I shiver, not from fear, but anticipation. The club's pulsing rhythm fades to a dull roar as Marcus's presence consumes me. His warning echoes in my mind, but I can't bring myself to heed it.

"I've never been one for caution," I murmur, leaning closer. The scent of his cologne—dark and spicy—envelops me.

Marcus's lips quirk, a ghost of a smile. "No, I don't imagine you are." His eyes rake over me, assessing. "It's late. Allow me to drive you home."

My heart skips. "I'd like that."

We weave through the crowd, his hand at the small of my back, guiding me. The cool night air hits my flushed skin as we step outside. Marcus leads me to a sleek black car, opening the door.

As we drive, the city lights blur into a hazy glow. Silence stretches between us, electric and taut. I steal glances at his profile, sharp and shadowed.

"You're playing with fire, Alana," Marcus says softly, eyes fixed on the road.

I turn to face him fully. "Maybe I want to burn."

His knuckles whiten on the steering wheel. We stop at a red light, and he turns to me, gaze searing. I feel myself gravitating towards him, drawn by an invisible force.

"You have no idea what you're asking for," he breathes, voice low and dangerous.

"Then enlighten me," I challenge, heart racing.

The light turns green. Marcus accelerates, the engine purring. We're speeding towards something inevitable, and I'm powerless to stop it.

The car slows to a stop outside my building. Silence descends, heavy and expectant. I turn to Marcus, my breath catching as I find him already watching me, his blue eyes dark with barely restrained desire.

"This is me," I whisper, but make no move to leave.

Marcus's hand reaches out, fingers grazing my cheek. "Alana," he murmurs, my name a prayer and a warning on his lips.

I lean into his touch, pulse quickening. "Yes?"

In one fluid motion, he pulls me close. Our lips meet, and the world falls away. The kiss is scorching, desperate, filled with a hunger that threatens to consume us both. His fingers tangle in my hair as mine clutch at his shirt, anchoring myself to him.

When we break apart, I'm gasping, dizzy

with want. Marcus rests his forehead against mine, his breath ragged.

"We shouldn't," he says, but his arms tighten around me.

I close my eyes, lost in the intoxicating warmth of him. "Why not?"

"Because once I start, I won't be able to stop," Marcus growls, the words sending a shiver down my spine.

Opening my eyes, I meet his gaze, seeing my own longing reflected there. "Then don't stop," I breathe, sealing our fates with another kiss.

Marcus pulls back, eyes blazing with barely controlled desire. "Alana," he warns, voice rough. "You don't understand what you're asking for."

"Then show me," I challenge, heart racing.

A low growl rumbles in his chest. In one fluid motion, he pulls me into his lap, hands gripping my hips. His lips crash against mine, hungry and demanding. I gasp, and he takes advantage, deepening the kiss.

"You're playing with fire," he murmurs against my neck, leaving a trail of scorching kisses. "I'll destroy you."

His words send a thrill through me. I arch into him, craving more. "Promise?" I breathe.

Marcus's eyes darken. "Oh, I promise." His hands roam my body, leaving trails of heat in their wake. "You have no idea the things I want to do to you."

I shiver with anticipation, lost in the intoxicating feeling of his touch. The world outside fades away until there's nothing but Marcus, his intoxicating scent, and the inferno building between us.

Marcus's hands grip my thighs, fingers digging into soft flesh as he pulls me flush against him. I can feel his hardness straining against his trousers, and I grind down, eliciting a low groan from his throat.

"Fuck, Alana," he growls, nipping at my earlobe. "Last chance to turn back."

"No, I want this," I gasp, desire pooling in my core. God, do I want this. I want it more than I've ever wanted anything in my entire life.

In a flash, he has the passenger seat reclined, laying me back as he hovers over me. His eyes glint with primal hunger as he takes in my disheveled state—dress hiked up, hair mussed, lips swollen from his kisses.

"You're a goddamn vision," Marcus rasps, trailing a hand up my thigh. "I'm going to *ruin* you for all other men."

His fingers brush against my lace panties, and I buck my hips, seeking more. He chuckles darkly, the sound vibrating through me.

"So eager," he taunts, dragging a finger along my clothed slit. "Is this all for me, babygirl?"

"Yes," I whimper, writhing beneath his touch. "Please, Marcus..."

"Please what?" he demands, pressing down on my clit. "Use your words, Alana. Tell me what you need."

Pride be damned, I'm too far gone to hold back. "I need you to fuck me," I beg, grinding against his hand. "I want you inside me. Make me yours."

Something dangerous flashes in Marcus's eyes, and then he's ripping my panties away, the delicate lace shredding under his impatient hands. Cool air hits my heated flesh, and I cry out, arching off the seat.

"Look at you, so fucking wet for me already," he growls appreciatively, dragging a finger through my slick folds. "You're dripping, babygirl."

Before I can respond, he thrusts two fingers inside me, curling them just right. I nearly scream at the sudden fullness, clenching around him.

"That's it," Marcus coaxes, pumping his fingers. "Take what I give you. Goddamn, you're tight. I can't wait to feel this sweet cunt wrapped around my cock."

His filthy words only heighten my arousal, and I rock my hips to meet his thrusts, chasing the building pressure. Marcus's thumb finds my clit, rubbing merciless circles that have me seeing stars.

"I'm close," I gasp, teetering on the edge. "Don't stop, please..."

"Come for me, Alana," he commands, curling his fingers deep. "Soak my hand. Let go."

His permission is my undoing. I shatter with a cry, my walls fluttering wildly around his fingers as wave after wave of ecstasy crashes over me. Marcus works me through it, drawing out my pleasure until I'm a trembling, mewling mess beneath him.

As I float down from the high, he withdraws his fingers, bringing them to his lips. His tongue darts out, lapping up my essence, and he groans appreciatively. "Delicious," he rumbles, eyes blazing with lust. "But I'm far from done with you."

In one smooth motion, Marcus frees his straining erection, and my mouth goes dry at the sight. He's long and thick, the engorged head already weeping with precum. I lick my lips unconsciously, suddenly desperate to taste him.

As if reading my mind, Marcus tangles his fingers in my hair, guiding me forward. "Open up, babygirl," he coaxes, tapping his cock against my lips. "Take what you need."

I part my lips eagerly, and he slides into the wet heat of my mouth with a low groan. The weight of him on my tongue is exquisite, and I hollow my cheeks, sucking hard. Marcus hisses in pleasure, grip tightening in my hair.

"Fuck, just like that," he praises, rocking his hips. "Your mouth was made for my cock."

Emboldened, I relax my jaw, taking him deeper. His length hits the back of my throat, and I gag slightly, but the discomfort only heightens my arousal. Tears prick at the corners of my eyes as I struggle to accommodate his girth, but I don't stop, determined to take all of him.

"Look at you, choking on my dick like the greedy little slut you are," Marcus growls, thrusting shallowly. "You love this, don't you? Being used for my pleasure?"

I can only moan in response, the vibrations making him twitch in my mouth. My own need is building again, my clit throbbing in time with each bob of my head. I snake a hand between my legs, desperate for friction.

Marcus notices, chuckling darkly. "Getting off on sucking my cock, babygirl? Go on then, touch yourself. Make yourself come while I fuck your pretty face."

Permission granted, I rub furious circles on my clit, hurtling towards another peak. Above me, Marcus's thrusts grow erratic, his breathing labored.

"I'm close," he warns, voice strained. "Where do you want it?"

I pull off him with a lewd pop, gasping for air. "On my face," I beg shamelessly, too far gone to care. "Mark me. Make me yours."

"Fuck, Alana," Marcus snarls, fisting his cock furiously. With a guttural groan, he comes, painting my face with thick ropes of his seed. The hot splash of it against my skin tips me over the edge, and I convulse with my own release, Marcus's name a broken prayer on my lips.

Panting, I collapse back against the seat, my body still trembling with aftershocks. Marcus looms over me, his eyes dark with satisfaction as he surveys his handiwork. With a gentleness that belies his earlier roughness, he swipes a thumb across my cheek, collecting a stray drop of his essence.

"Look at you," he murmurs, voice low and gravelly. "Debauched and beautiful. Wearing my cum like a badge of honor."

I shiver at his words, a fresh wave of desire cresting despite my satiated state. What is it about this man? I *crave* him with an intensity that should scare me.

Marcus tucks himself away, righting his clothes with an ease that speaks of practice. I feel a pang of jealousy at the thought of him doing this with other women, but I quickly tamp it down. I have no claim on him, no right to such feelings.

As if sensing my thoughts, Marcus leans in,

his lips brushing the shell of my ear. "Don't worry, babygirl," he whispers, sending a thrill down my spine. "You're the only one I want. The only one who can take me like this."

I turn my head, capturing his lips in a searing kiss. He groans into my mouth, hands coming up to frame my face as he deepens the kiss, consuming me.

When we finally break apart, both of us are breathing hard. Marcus rests his forehead against mine, eyes closed.

Finally, Marcus pulls back, his mask slipping back into place. "You should go," he says, voice carefully neutral. "Before I decide to keep you here all night."

I nod, not trusting my voice. With shaky hands, I straighten my dress, trying to make myself presentable. Marcus watches me, a glimmer of amusement in his eyes.

"Goodbye, Alana," he murmurs as I reach for the door handle.

I pause, glancing back at him over my shoulder, a sliver of panic slicing through me. "Will I see you again?"

His lips curve into a dangerous smile. "Oh, you're mine now, little one."

My heart trips at the look on his face.

The door closes, but I can feel his gaze on me as I enter my apartment.

He doesn't leave until I'm inside.

It's only when I'm inside that my senses come back to me and I wonder if I should have heeded his warning to stay away from him.

CHAPTER 2

The shadows of my past curl around me like smoke, choking out the light. I stare at my reflection in the mirror, but Marcus's piercing blue eyes stare back. His gaze haunts me, a ghost I can't exorcise.

"Get out of my head," I whisper, fingers trembling as I grip the sink.

But the memories flood in, unbidden. His voice, low and dangerous. The electricity when our hands brushed. The way he looked at me like he could see right through to my soul.

I splash cold water on my face, willing the thoughts away. It doesn't work. Nothing works.

My phone chimes. A news alert. I grab it, desperate for distraction.

The headline stops my breath:

Marcus Blackwood: Entrepreneur or Criminal Mastermind?

My heart pounds as I scan the article. Words jump out at me.

Suspected ties to organized crime. Money laundering. Person of interest in ongoing investigation.

"It can't be true," I murmur.

But a small voice whispers: *What if it is?*

I think of Marcus's calculating gaze, the careful way he chose his words. The hint of danger that clung to him like a second skin.

My finger hovers over the link to read more. Do I dare? Do I want to know the truth?

The shadows press closer, urging me on. My curiosity burns, insatiable. With a shaky breath, I tap the screen.

As I read, a chill creeps down my spine. Each word paints a darker picture of the man who's consumed my thoughts. Yet I can't look away. I'm drawn in, caught in Marcus's web.

"What have I gotten myself into?" I whisper to the empty room.

But deep down, I know it's already too late to turn back.

———

The harsh fluorescent lights of the office flicker, casting writhing shadows across my desk. I blink, trying to focus on the mockup before me. My mind wanders, lost in a labyrinth of questions about Marcus.

A hush falls over the room. The air grows thick, oppressive. I look up.

He's here.

Marcus stands in the doorway, a dark silhouette against the sterile white walls. My breath catches. He moves towards me with predatory grace, each step deliberate.

"Alana," he says, voice low and smooth as velvet. "I hope I'm not interrupting."

I swallow hard, my heart galloping away in my chest at the sight of him. "What are you doing here?"

A ghost of a smile plays on his lips. "I was in the neighborhood. Thought I'd drop by."

My colleagues stare, curious whispers rippling through the office. I feel exposed, vulnerable.

"Coffee?" Marcus asks, but it's not really a question.

I nod, numb. We walk to the nearby café in tense silence. The aroma of roasted beans does nothing to calm my racing heart.

Once seated, I find my voice. "Why are you really here, Marcus?"

He leans back, studying me. "Perhaps I simply wanted to see you again."

"Cut the cryptic act," I snap. "I know about your...connections."

A flicker of something—surprise? amusement?—crosses his face. "Do you now?"

I press on. "The article. Your criminal ties. Is it true?"

Marcus takes a slow sip of coffee. "The world isn't black and white, Alana. You of all people should understand that."

"What's that supposed to mean?"

He leans forward, eyes boring into mine. "We all have secrets. Shadows we'd rather keep hidden."

A chill runs down my spine. Does he know about my past?

"You didn't answer my question," I persist.

Marcus's laugh is cold, mirthless. "Some

questions are better left unanswered. For both our sakes."

I shake my head, frustration building. "I deserve the truth."

"Truth?" he murmurs. "Be careful what you wish for, Alana. Once seen, it can't be unseen."

His words hang in the air, heavy with unspoken threats and dark promises. I should walk away. I know I should.

But I can't. The shadows of my own past reach out, entangling with his. I'm caught in his web, and part of me doesn't want to break free.

I rise abruptly, needing space, air. But Marcus is there, crowding me against the wall, his presence overwhelming. The scent of his cologne—rich, dark, intoxicating—fills my senses.

"Running again?" he murmurs, voice low and dangerous.

I swallow hard. "I'm not running. I just...I need to think."

His eyes, stormy blue, search mine. "What are you so afraid of, Alana?"

"I'm not afraid," I lie, my voice barely a whisper.

A sardonic smile plays on his lips. "Aren't you?"

His hand brushes my cheek, feather-light. I shiver, torn between desire and dread.

"This...us...it's not a good idea," I manage.

"I know," he agrees. "I told you when we first met. I warned you to stay away from me, told you I wasn't a good man, but you, you little prying Pandora, had to open the box."

I close my eyes, willing myself to resist. But my traitorous heart betrays me, pounding a staccato rhythm against my ribs.

"I should go," I breathe.

Marcus leans in, his lips ghosting my ear. "You should, but you won't."

A knock at the door shatters the moment. My friend Jenna's voice filters through.

"Alana? You in there?"

Marcus steps back, his mask of cool indifference sliding seamlessly back into place.

"Until later, babygirl," he murmurs, before slipping out a side door.

Jenna enters, her brow furrowed with concern. "Was that Marcus Blackwood I just saw?"

I nod, still reeling.

"Alana, you need to be careful," she warns. "That man is dangerous."

But even as she speaks, I feel the pull. The

siren song of secrets and shadows, of a world I both fear and crave.

"I know," I whisper. But the words ring hollow, even to my own ears.

———

The city night presses against my windows, a suffocating shroud. I pace my apartment, Marcus's words echoing in my mind like a haunting refrain. My phone chirps—a message. Unknown number.

Heart racing, I open it:

> Stay away from Marcus Blackwood. For your own safety.

A chill slithers down my spine. I type with trembling fingers:

> Who is this?

No response. The silence mocks me.

I sink onto my couch, the leather cool against my feverish skin. "What have I gotten myself into?" I whisper to the empty room.

My reflection in the darkened TV screen

looks ghostly, unfamiliar. Is that really me? The woman teetering on the edge of...what? Danger? Passion? Destruction?

The phone buzzes again. I snatch it up, but it's only Jenna:

> You okay? Still thinking about
> what I said?

I start to type "I'm fine," but delete it. Lies taste bitter now.

> I don't know what to think
> anymore.

My gaze drifts to the window. In the glass, for just a moment, I swear I see a figure watching from the street below. Dark, imposing. Familiar.

I blink, and it's gone.

"Marcus," I breathe, "what game are you playing?"

The night offers no answers, only the promise of secrets yet to be unraveled.

CHAPTER 3

The limousine glides to a stop, a sleek predator in the night. Marcus emerges first, his hand extended. I hesitate before taking it, feeling the warmth of his skin against my own.

I shouldn't be here. Shouldn't have come with him when he showed up to my apartment and demanded I join him for dinner.

But I can't resist him, it seems, so here I am.

"Alana," he murmurs, "welcome to La Lune Noire."

The restaurant materializes from the shadows—a Victorian mansion, windows glowing with soft candlelight. As we approach, I catch glimpses of ornate wallpaper, crystal chandeliers. My heart quickens.

"It's beautiful," I breathe.

Marcus's lips curl into a smile that doesn't reach his eyes. "Beauty can be deceiving."

Inside, we're led to a secluded alcove draped in deep crimson. Marcus pulls out my chair, his fingers brushing my shoulder. Electricity crackles between us.

"You seem tense," I observe as he takes his seat.

He sighs, running a hand through his dark hair. "Perhaps I am. It's been...a trying week."

"Do you want to talk about it?"

His piercing blue eyes lock onto mine. "Are you sure you want to hear?"

I nod, leaning forward. "I'm a good listener."

Marcus is quiet for a long moment. When he speaks, his voice is low, haunted. "My past is not a pretty thing, Alana. There are shadows there, sins that cling to me like a second skin."

A chill races down my spine. Part of me wants to flee, to escape whatever darkness lurks behind his words. But a larger part is drawn in, mesmerized.

"We all have regrets," I say softly.

He laughs, a harsh sound. "Regrets? No. What I carry goes beyond mere regret."

The waiter appears, pouring blood-red

wine. Marcus watches the liquid swirl in his glass. "When I was young, I made choices. Terrible choices that seemed right at the time. But their consequences..." He trails off, lost in memory.

I reach across the table, my fingers grazing his. "You don't have to tell me everything. Not if you're not ready."

His eyes meet mine again, filled with a pain that makes my chest ache. "No," he says, his mask slipping back into place, his voice turning neutral.

And just like that, he's hard again, any earlier trace of vulnerability gone.

The low, sultry notes of a jazz melody weave through the air as Marcus takes my hand, leading me to the dance floor. His touch sends electricity coursing through my veins. We move together, bodies swaying in perfect synchronicity.

"You dance beautifully," I murmur, my heart racing.

Marcus's lips curve into a half-smile, his eyes never leaving mine. "It's all about finding the right partner."

His hand on my lower back pulls me closer, and I can feel the heat radiating from his body.

The scent of his cologne—dark and spicy— envelops me. We're so close now, I can see the faint stubble on his jawline, the intensity burning in his gaze.

As we turn, I catch a glimpse of other patrons watching us. Their stares prickle my skin, but Marcus seems oblivious to everything but me.

"What are you thinking?" I ask, trying to decipher the emotions flickering across his face.

He hesitates, his grip tightening almost imperceptibly. "That I'm playing a dangerous game," he says finally, his voice low and rough.

The music swells, and he dips me suddenly. As he brings me back up, our faces are inches apart. For a moment, I think he might kiss me. Instead, he whispers, "Come home with me, Alana."

My breath catches in my throat. It's not a question, but I whisper "yes" anyway, barely audible.

The ride to his penthouse is a blur of antici- pation and unspoken tension. As we step inside, the city lights sprawl out below us through floor-to-ceiling windows. Marcus moves to pour us drinks, his movements graceful yet taut with some hidden strain.

"There's something I need to tell you," he says, handing me a glass. His eyes are shadowed, conflicted. "The life I lead, the choices I've made—they've created enemies. Dangerous ones."

Fear prickles my spine. I take a slow sip, studying him. "Why are you telling me this?"

He runs a hand through his hair, a rare gesture of vulnerability. "Because I'm selfish enough to want you in my life, even knowing it could put you at risk."

The glass in my hand suddenly feels heavy. Part of me screams to run, to flee this beautiful, dangerous man and the world he inhabits. But a deeper, darker part whispers that it's already too late—I'm already ensnared.

Marcus sees the look on my face, and his eyes darken. "I tried to warn you," he growls.

I turn away, but he snatches me back to him. His body is pressed flush against my back, and his hand comes up to cup my throat threateningly. "I knew once I had my hands on you, it would spark an obsession I can't ignore," he hisses in my ear. "Knew you would be *mine*."

He spins me back around and forces me to look at him. His eyes blaze down at me with an almost unhinged, feral look. "Kiss me like a good girl," he demands, but he doesn't give me time to take the initiative before his lips crash onto mine, urgent and demanding.

I surrender to the kiss, to the intoxicating blend of danger and desire that Marcus embodies. Our clothes fall away, barriers crumbling like sand castles before the tide.

I catch glimpses of scars on his skin—stories etched in flesh. I trace them with trembling fingers, wondering at the pain they represent.

"Don't ask," Marcus murmurs, his voice a rough warning.

And then he's inside me with one sharp thrust. I gasp, the sudden fullness, pain bordering on pleasure.

He groans, a deep sound of primal male satisfaction that has me instnatly wet.

His hands tighten on my hips as he thrusts into me, each stroke more forceful than the last. I gasp, my nails raking down his sweat-slicked back. The pleasure borders on pain, teetering on that razor's edge.

Without warning, Marcus flips me onto my stomach, his weight pressing me into the mattress. I hear the snick of a switchblade and freeze, heart pounding. The cold metal traces the curve of my spine, not breaking skin but promising it could.

"Do you trust me, Alana?" His voice is a dark purr in my ear.

I should say no. Should flee this beautiful, deadly man and never look back. But instead I arch into his touch, a breathless "yes" escaping my lips.

The blade dances over my skin, leaving goosebumps in its wake. It dips lower, skimming the swell of my buttocks. I shiver, equal parts fear and anticipation.

"Good girl," Marcus growls approvingly. The knife disappears and he grips my hips, slamming into me with renewed force. I cry out, fingers twisting in the sheets.

He leans down, his chest warm against my back, his breath hot on my neck. "You're perfect for me," he rasps. "Knew it the moment I first saw you. So innocent, so tempting. Begging to be corrupted."

His words send heat rushing through me, stoking the flames of my desire. I moan, pushing back against him wantonly.

Suddenly his hand is in my hair, yanking my head back. The knife is back too, the point dimpling the delicate skin beneath my jaw. I go still, hardly daring to breathe.

"You're mine now," Marcus snarls, punctuating his words with a sharp thrust that makes me gasp. "No other man can ever touch you. I'll kill anyone who tries. Do you understand?"

Tears sting my eyes, but I'm not sure if they're from fear or the overwhelming intensity of my arousal. "Yes," I manage to choke out.

"Say it." The command is laced with unspoken threat.

"I'm yours."

With a harsh groan, he releases me, sheathing the knife and tossing it aside. His hands gentle, he turns me back over and kisses me deeply, tenderly. The contrast leaves me reeling.

I feel his cock pulse inside me.

Marcus's thrusts grow more forceful, claiming me with each intense stroke. I'm lost in the overwhelming sensations—the drag of his skin against mine, the taste of him on my tongue, the dark promises he whispers.

"Let go, Alana," he commands, his voice tight with strain. "Surrender to me."

And I do. The coil of tension inside me snaps and I shatter around him, my release hitting with the force of a tsunami. I cry out, my nails scoring his back, my body convulsing.

Marcus follows me over the edge with a guttural groan, his hips snapping forward one final time. I feel his release, hot and pulsing, deep inside me.

Claiming me.

For a long moment, we remain locked together, chests heaving, sweat cooling on our entangled limbs. Marcus holds me after, stroking my hair as I tremble in his arms. He brushes a damp strand of hair from my face, his touch unexpectedly gentle.

"You are exquisite," he murmurs, pressing a kiss to my temple.

I want to respond, but exhaustion drags at me, my eyelids growing heavy. The last thing I remember before sleep claims me is the possessive curl of Marcus's body around mine, shielding me even as he imprisons me.

———

Dawn breaks, pale light creeping across the sky. I blink awake, disoriented. The bed beside me is empty, the sheets cold. Marcus is gone.

Panic claws at my throat as I sit up, scan

ning the room. No note, no sign of where he's gone or when he'll return. The penthouse feels suddenly vast and alien, a gilded cage.

I wrap the sheet around myself, padding to the window. The city below stirs to life, oblivious to my turmoil. What game is Marcus playing? And more importantly, what role have I cast myself in?

I turn from the window, a chill creeping up my spine despite the warmth of the morning sun. My eyes dart around the room, searching for...something. A clue, an explanation, anything to make sense of this surreal situation.

That's when I see it. A folded piece of paper on the nightstand, stark white against the dark wood. My heart pounds as I reach for it with trembling fingers.

"Alana," it reads in Marcus's bold script, "Do not try to leave. I have a man stationed outside the door. He will stop you if you try."

The words swim before my eyes. Am I a prisoner now?

My mind races, fragments of last night flashing through my thoughts. Marcus's cryptic words about his past, the intensity in his eyes when he spoke of danger. I'd been too caught up in the moment, too intoxicated by his presence to truly hear the warning in his words.

Now, holding this note, the full weight of my naivety crashes down upon me. I've stumbled into something far beyond my depth, a world of shadows and secrets that threatens to swallow me whole.

"God, what have I done?" The words escape me in a choked sob.

I clutch the note to my chest, torn between the urge to flee and a perverse desire to unravel this mystery, to understand the man who's captured my heart and my imagination so completely.

The city beckons beyond the window, familiar and safe. Yet even as I contemplate escape, I know a part of me has already been irreversibly changed. The Alana who walked into that restaurant last night no longer exists.

What have I gotten myself into? And more importantly, how do I extricate myself from the dark web that Marcus has woven around me?

CHAPTER 4

The door slams open. Marcus looms in the doorway, a dark silhouette against the fading light. My fury ignites.

"Why have you made me a prisoner?" I demand, fists clenched at my sides.

His eyes flash dangerously as he stalks toward me. "Because you're mine now, Alana."

The growl in his voice sends a shiver down my spine—fear or desire, I can't tell. Perhaps both.

"I belong to no one," I spit back, even as my heart races.

He grabs my wrist, his touch electric. "We're leaving. Now."

I want to resist, to fight, but some invisible force compels me to follow as he drags me from the room. We emerge into the twilight, the air heavy with the scent of coming rain. A sleek black car waits, engine purring.

As we drive through darkening streets, Marcus's jaw clenches and unclenches. The silence stretches, taut as a bowstring.

"Where are you taking me?" I finally ask, hating the tremor in my voice.

"Home," he says simply.

We pass through wrought iron gates, winding up a long drive flanked by gnarled old trees. A massive stone manor looms ahead, windows glowing like eyes in the gloom.

Marcus's knuckles whiten on the steering wheel. "I grew up here," he says, voice hollow. "Surrounded by violence and loss."

The words hang in the air between us. I peer at his profile, seeing for the first time the haunted look in his eyes. What ghosts linger here, I wonder? And will they claim me too?

The gravel crunches beneath our feet as we walk the sprawling grounds. Mist clings to the manicured hedges, obscuring the edges of this gilded prison. Marcus's shoulder brushes mine, sending electricity crackling through my veins.

"My father built an empire on blood and

lies," he murmurs, eyes fixed on some distant point. "Every room in that house holds a secret."

I shiver, not entirely from the chill. "What kind of secrets?"

He turns to me, his gaze piercing. "The kind that destroy lives, Alana. The kind that haunt you."

We pause before a weathered stone bench. Marcus traces the engraved surface with long fingers. "This is where I found my mother. After she..."

He doesn't finish. He doesn't need to. The weight of unspoken tragedy hangs heavy in the air.

"Why are you telling me this?" I whisper.

His laugh is bitter, sharp as broken glass. "Because you need to understand what you've walked into."

"Then why not let me go?" I ask softly even as my heart balks at the idea.

His eyes blaze at me with fury. "Because I can't now. Don't you get it? You've emblazoned yourself on my soul, Alana."

My breath catches at the almost manic look in his eyes.

He looks away, and when his eyes meet mine again, they're neutral again. His violent mood swings should scare me. They halfway do.

Thunder rumbles in the distance as we make our way back to the house. Marcus leads me down a dim hallway, stopping before an ornate door. He hesitates, hand on the knob.

"This was my father's study," he says, voice tight. "No one's been inside since..."

The door creaks open, revealing a room frozen in time. The air is thick with dust and secrets. Marcus's breathing grows ragged as he steps inside. I follow, drawn by a morbid curiosity I can't explain.

"You shouldn't be here," he growls, but makes no move to stop me.

The tension crackles between us, electric and dangerous. I can feel the weight of his gaze, heavy with unspoken desire and barely restrained violence. My heart pounds, a mix of fear and something darker, something I'm afraid to name.

I turn to face Marcus, my pulse racing. The room feels too small, too charged with unspoken truths. I can't bear it any longer.

"Why me?" I demand, my voice trembling. "Of all the people in the world, why am I here?"

Marcus's eyes darken, storm clouds gathering. He takes a step closer, and I fight the urge to retreat.

"You really want to know?" His voice is low, dangerous.

I nod, unable to speak.

"Because you're not afraid," he says, closing the distance between us. "Everyone else cowers or simpers. But you...you look right through me."

His hand comes up, fingers ghosting along my jawline. I shiver, caught between desire and dread.

"I see a strength in you, Alana," he murmurs. "A fire that matches my own. It calls to me. Haunts me."

I swallow hard, lost in the intensity of his gaze. "And what if I don't want to be called?"

A smile plays at the corners of his mouth, sharp as a blade. "Then why are you still here?"

He's right. I could have run. Should have run. But something keeps me rooted to this spot, drawn to the darkness that surrounds him like a shroud.

Marcus leans in, his breath hot against my ear. "Tell me to stop," he whispers.

I don't. I *can't*. The words stick in my throat

as his lips brush mine, igniting a fire that threatens to consume us both.

His hands roam my body, possessive and demanding, as if he has every right to claim me. And in this moment, I'm powerless to resist.

Marcus pushes me against the wall, and I gasp as his hand leaves a stinging warmth on my bottom. "Tell me your secrets," he growls.

Fear and arousal mingle within me, fueling the blaze between my thighs. My breath comes in pants as he spanks me again, harder this time.

"I... I-I...," I stammer, fighting to find the words.

He pauses, his blue eyes boring into mine. "Tell me, Alana. Or I stop."

The ultimatum hangs between us, heavy as the air itself. In the end, it is the look in his eyes that undoes me—the faintest flicker of desolation, so like my own.

"Fine," I grit out, "I...I killed him."

"Who?" he asks, though his eyes says he already knows.

"My father." And then the words rush out of me, a confession long overdue. Marcus's hand freezes, his body rigid against mine. Slowly, he turns me to face him, his eyes searching mine for any sign of deception.

"Why?" he asks, voice barely a whisper.

And so, I tell him. I confess my darkest sin, the night I ended a life to save my own. "He was a bastard, and he hurt me long enough. I don't regret it," I tell him defiantly.

My voice shakes with the weight of the memory, but Marcus doesn't flinch away. Instead, he pulls me closer, his hands roaming my body once more, but this time, it's to soothe, to heal. "It's over now," he whispers, his voice a balm to my fractured soul. "You're safe here."

In that moment, I believe him. As his lips find mine again, I allow myself to sink into the depths of our twisted connection, two lost souls clinging to each other in the darkness.

Marcus's touch grows more insistent, more demanding. His hands roam my body, claiming every inch as his own. I moan as he palms my breasts, my nipples hardening under his touch.

"You're mine," he growls, his voice thick with desire. "Say it."

"I'm yours," I gasp, the words torn from my throat.

He rewards me with a searing kiss, his tongue plundering my mouth. I cling to him, my nails digging into his shoulders as he grinds his hardness against me.

"I know what you need, babygirl," he tells me.

Suddenly, he spins me around, bending me over the heavy oak desk. I cry out as he yanks up my skirt, exposing my bare bottom to the cool air. His hand comes down hard, the sharp sting sending shockwaves through my body.

My mouth opens in a silent gasp. I'm so shocked.

"Count," he commands, his voice brooking no argument.

I try to pull away, the embarassment and degradation causing my cheeks to heat, but he holds me firmly, his voice brooking no argument as he repeats himself, his voice like steel, "Count."

I grit my teeth, but obey. "One," I manage, my voice shaking.

Again and again, his hand cracks against my sensitive flesh. While the embarassment is still there, I'm surprised when the pain blurs into pleasure, each strike stoking the fire between my thighs. By the time we reach ten, I'm a writhing, desperate mess.

"Please," I beg, not even knowing what I'm asking for.

Marcus chuckles darkly, his fingers skimming the wet heat of my center. "Please what, Alana? Use your words."

"Please, I need you," I whimper, pushing back against his hand.

He tsks, withdrawing his touch. "Not yet. Not until I say."

I nearly sob with frustration, my body wound tight as a coiled spring. Marcus takes his time, his hands and mouth mapping every curve, every hollow. He brings me to the brink again and again, only to pull back, leaving me teetering on the edge.

"Marcus, please," I pant, my pride long since abandoned. "I can't take it anymore."

He leans over me, his chest pressed to my back. "Then let go, Alana. Come for me."

His words are my undoing. I shatter without a touch. It's just the force of his words, my body convulsing with the force of my release. I've never experienced anything like it. Wave after wave crashes over me, dragging me under. Through it all, Marcus holds me, whispering praise of what a good girl I am, his touch gentling as I slowly drift back to earth.

When I finally catch my breath, he turns me to face him, his blue eyes soft with something that looks dangerously like affection. He brushes a strand of hair from my face, his touch almost reverent.

"You're beautiful when you let go," he murmurs.

I blush, suddenly self-conscious under the intensity of his gaze. "Marcus, I..."

He silences me with a kiss, slow and deep. When he pulls back, there's a new resolve in his eyes.

"We can't stay here," he says, his voice urgent. "It's not safe. For either of us."

I nod, understanding now the weight he carries.

We hurry through the darkened halls of the estate, Marcus's hand gripping mine tightly. The air is thick with tension, our footsteps echoing off the cold marble floors. As we emerge into the night, a chill wind whips through my hair, carrying with it a sense of foreboding.

Marcus ushers me towards the waiting car, his eyes scanning the shadows. Suddenly, the silence is shattered by the crack of gunfire.

Instinctively, Marcus shoves me behind him, shielding me with his body.

"Stay down," he growls, reaching for the gun holstered at his side.

My heart pounds in my chest as I crouch behind the car door, watching as Marcus moves with lethal grace. The moonlight glints off the blade in his hand, and I catch a glimpse of his face—cold, focused, utterly ruthless.

The attackers emerge from the darkness, their faces obscured by black masks. Marcus doesn't hesitate. He lunges forward, his knife flashing in a silver arc. Blood sprays, black in the moonlight, as he slits the first man's throat with one swift motion.

I should be horrified, sickened by the violence unfolding before me. But as I watch Marcus move, a dark thrill unfurls within me. There's a savage beauty to his brutality, a raw power that sets my blood on fire.

The second attacker falls just as quickly, his scream cut short as Marcus's blade finds his heart. The third manages to land a blow, his fist connecting with Marcus's jaw. But Marcus barely flinches. He retaliates with a flurry of strikes, his movements a blur of speed and precision. In seconds, the man crumples to the ground, his neck twisted at an unnatural angle.

And then it's over. The silence returns, broken only by Marcus's ragged breathing. He turns to me, his eyes wild, blood splattered across his face and hands. I know I should be repulsed, should recoil from the monster before me.

But I don't. Instead, I step towards him, drawn by an irresistible force. My hand reaches up to touch his face, my fingers trailing through the slick wetness of blood. Marcus's eyes flutter closed for a moment, leaning into my touch like a man starved for affection.

When his eyes open again, they blaze with a different kind of hunger. He pulls me to him roughly, his mouth crashing down on mine in a bruising kiss. I can taste the metallic tang of blood on his tongue, and it only fuels the dark desire coursing through my veins.

His hands roam my body, leaving smears of red in their wake. There's a frantic urgency to his touch, as if he needs to reassure himself that I'm real, that I'm alive. I melt into him, my own hands clutching at his shoulders, nails digging into his flesh. The world around us fades away until nothing exists but the heat of our bodies, the pounding of our hearts.

Marcus breaks the kiss, his forehead resting against mine. "We need to go," he pants, his breath hot against my skin. "More will come."

I nod, not trusting my voice. He takes my hand, leading me to the car. As we speed off into the night, I glance back at the shadowy estate, the bodies littering the ground. I should feel horror, remorse. But all I feel is a grim satisfaction, a sense of inevitability.

This is my life now, intertwined with Marcus's. There's no going back, no pretending we're anything other than what we are—two damaged souls, bound by blood and secrets.

The city lights blur past the window as we race through the sleeping streets. Marcus's hand rests on my thigh, his touch possessive, grounding. I lean my head against his shoulder, exhaustion settling deep in my bones.

"Sleep," he murmurs, his lips brushing my temple. "I'll keep you safe."

As I drift off, lulled by the purr of the engine and the warmth of Marcus's body, a final thought flickers through my mind. Perhaps this is what love is, in a world where innocence is lost and trust is a luxury we cannot afford. A love as sharp as a blade, as unyielding as the ties that bind us.

A love written in blood and sealed with secrets, destined to consume us both.

CHAPTER 5

The safe house looms before us, a decrepit Victorian mansion with peeling paint and shuttered windows. As Marcus ushers me inside, musty air fills my lungs. We're trapped here now, just the two of us in this decaying tomb.

"It's not much, but it'll keep you hidden," Marcus says, his voice echoing in the empty foyer.

I nod, unable to speak. The walls seem to close in, suffocating me with their moldering wallpaper and faded memories. What sins lie buried in the foundations of this place?

We climb creaking stairs to the second floor. Marcus leads me to a small bedroom, its furnishings draped in ghostly sheets. "You'll stay here," he says. "I'll be down the hall."

So close, yet so far. The thought sends a shiver down my spine.

A whistle pierces the silence. One of Marcus's men leans in the doorway, leering at me. "Nice piece of ass you've got there, boss," he drawls. "Mind if I have a taste?"

Before I can react, Marcus's fist connects with the man's jaw. He crumples to the floor as Marcus looms over him, eyes blazing with cold fury.

"If you ever speak about her like that again," Marcus snarls, "I'll cut your balls off myself. Understood?"

The man nods frantically, scrambling away.

I stand frozen, heart pounding.

My voice trembles as I break the oppressive silence. "Marcus, that...that was over the top."

He whirls on me, his blue eyes stormy. "Oh? Did you prefer his attention, Alana?"

The accusation stings, igniting a fire in my chest. Without thinking, I slap him, the crack echoing through the dusty room.

Marcus catches my wrist, his grip firm but not painful. For a heartbeat, we're suspended in time, the air crackling with tension. Then he pulls me close, crashing his lips against mine.

The kiss is savage, desperate. I taste whiskey and danger on his tongue. My fingers tangle in his dark hair as he pushes me against the wall, his body hard against mine.

"I'll show you just who you belong to," he growls against my neck.

His touch ignites a feverish desire within me, a tempest of lust and loathing. We tear at each other's clothes, buttons popping and fabric ripping, baring our sins to the stale air. Marcus's hands roam my body, possessive and demanding, as if he can brand his fingerprints onto my very soul.

I arch into him, nails raking down his back, leaving crimson trails of passion and pain. Our shadows dance a macabre waltz on the peeling walls as we lose ourselves in the darkness. The ancient bed creaks beneath our writhing bodies, a mocking chorus to our forbidden union.

Release crashes over me like a tidal wave, dragging me under into blissful oblivion. For a fleeting moment, I forget the horrors that await beyond these moldering walls. All that exists is the searing heat of Marcus's skin against mine, the thunder of his heart echoing my own.

But as we lie tangled in sweat-soaked sheets, reality seeps back in like a bone-chilling fog. This decaying mansion holds secrets, and so does the man beside me. I've stepped into a world of shadows and danger, and there may be no turning back.

Morning light filters through grimy windows, casting an eerie pallor over the room. I wake to an empty bed, the space beside me cold. Hushed voices drift from downstairs, and I creep to the landing, straining to listen.

Marcus's baritone rumbles, low and urgent. "I told you, I'll handle it. Just give me more time."

A pause, then a garbled response I can't make out. My heart pounds as I inch closer, floorboards groaning beneath my bare feet.

"It's done," he says, his tone clipped. "No one will find her here."

Ice floods my veins. They're talking about me. Secrets swirl in the stagnant air, taunting me with their elusive whispers. What is Marcus hiding?

"Keep it quiet," Marcus continues. "I don't care what it costs. Just make it happen."

I swallow hard, steeling myself as I step into the room. Marcus's eyes snap to mine, a flicker of something—surprise? anger?—crossing his face before it settles into its usual mask of cool detachment.

"Who were you talking to?" I ask, my voice steadier than I feel.

Marcus's jaw tightens. "Business," he says curtly, sliding his phone into his pocket.

"What kind of business involves hiding someone?" The words tumble out before I can stop them.

He moves towards me, each step deliberate. "Alana," he says, my name a warning on his lips. His eyes meet mine, stormy blue darkening to midnight. "Go back to bed."

But I stand my ground, even as my knees tremble. "Why? So you can keep more secrets from me? It's not fair, Marcus. You know everything about me, but I'm realizing I don't know you at all."

He takes another step towards me, his jaw clenched. "There are things you're better off not knowing. Trust me."

A bitter laugh escapes my lips. "Trust you? When you've done nothing but lie and evade since the moment we met?"

Marcus reaches for me, but I jerk away. "No more games. I want the truth, or I walk."

He runs a hand through his disheveled hair, a crack appearing in his calm facade before he suddenly throws me over his shoulder.

I gasp at the sudden movement and beat my fists against his back, but he acts like it doesn't hurt him at all. He slaps my ass and holds my legs down so I can't kick as he marches me back up the stairs and throws me down on the bed.

Then, fast as lighting, he's across the room. He slams the door behind him, and I hear a lock click.

I'm pissed as hell as I beat on the door. "Marcus, you bastard! Let me out!"

Of course, he doesn't.

CHAPTER 6

The door slams open. Marcus looms in the threshold, darkness clinging to him like a second skin. My anger flares anew at his nonchalant entrance after hours of waiting.

"Where were you?" I demand, voice trembling.

He doesn't answer, stalking toward me with predatory grace. Before I can protest, his lips crash against mine. I try to resist, to hold onto my fury, but it melts away like snow in summer. His kiss consumes me, igniting a fire I can't control.

Marcus growls against my mouth. "I need you. Now."

He shoves me against the wall, pinning my

wrists above my head. His teeth graze my neck, sending shivers down my spine. I gasp as he enters me in one swift thrust.

"Marcus, I—"

"Shh," he murmurs, biting down on my pulse point. "Just feel."

I'm helpless against the onslaught of sensation.

A whimper escapes my lips as he trails kisses down my throat, his stubble scraping deliciously against my skin. He releases my wrists, hands gliding over my curves with maddening slowness. My fingers tangle in his hair, urging him lower.

Marcus smirks up at me, blue eyes gleaming with dark promise. In one fluid motion, he rips open my blouse, buttons scattering across the floor. Cool air caresses my flushed skin before his scorching mouth descends on my breast. I cry out, back arching as he sucks a taut nipple between his teeth. Electric pleasure zings straight to my core.

"Please," I beg, not even sure what I'm asking for. More, more, more.

He lavishes attention on my other breast, tongue swirling, teeth nipping, stoking the inferno inside me higher. Just when I think I might combust from the exquisite torture, he pulls back. I whine at the loss of contact.

Before I can protest, Marcus scoops me up and tosses me onto the bed. I bounce once before he's on me again, settling between my thighs. His hardness presses insistently against my center, making me squirm with need.

"You're wearing too many clothes," he rasps.

I couldn't agree more. We make short work of the rest of our garments until we're skin to skin, nothing between us but charged air and pulsing desire. He nudges my legs further apart, exposing my dripping sex to his heated gaze.

"Beautiful," Marcus murmurs reverently. "And all mine."

Then his mouth is on me and I'm lost. His tongue delves into my folds, lapping at the evidence of my arousal. I fist the sheets, hips canting shamelessly against his face as he explores every slick inch of my core. He zeroes in on my clit, sucking the sensitive nub until stars explode behind my eyelids.

"Marcus!" I scream, thighs clamping around his head as I shatter.

Relentless, he works me through the after-shocks, coaxing out every last tremor of release. Only when I collapse bonelessly onto the mattress does he kiss his way back up my quivering body. He claims my mouth in a searing kiss, letting me taste myself on his tongue.

Marcus's rigid length glides along my inner thigh, leaving a glistening trail of precum in its wake. The slick sensation sends a fresh wave of desire coursing through my veins. He notches himself at my entrance, teasing me with the promise of fullness. I whimper, arching my back in a silent plea.

"Tell me what you want," he demands, voice rough with need.

"You," I gasp out. "I want you inside me. Please, Marcus..."

With an animalistic growl, he slams into me, filling me to the hilt in one brutal thrust. A strangled cry tears from my throat at the sudden intrusion. He stills for a moment, allowing me to adjust to his impressive girth stretching me wide.

Then he begins to move, setting a punishing pace that has the headboard slamming against the wall. Each powerful stroke hits a spot deep inside me, stoking the embers of my arousal into an inferno. I cling to his shoulders, nails raking down his back as he pistons in and out of my clenching heat.

"So tight," Marcus grunts, burying his face in the crook of my neck. "You feel incredible wrapped around my cock."

His filthy words only heighten my pleasure. I meet him thrust for thrust, legs locking around his waist to pull him impossibly deeper. The obscene sound of flesh slapping against flesh fills the room, mingling with our harsh pants and moans.

Suddenly, his hand wraps around my throat, applying just enough pressure to make my head spin deliciously. He squeezes slightly, controlling my air flow as he continues to pound into me mercilessly. The edges of my vision blur, intensifying every sensation. Electric tingles race across my skin, coalescing at the apex of my thighs where we're joined.

"That's it, baby," he coaxes darkly. "Give in to me. Let go."

His grip tightens fractionally and that's all it takes to send me hurtling over the edge into oblivion. My inner muscles clamp down on him viciously as ecstasy crashes over me in waves. I convulse beneath him, mouth open in a silent scream of rapture.

Seconds later, Marcus buries himself to the hilt with a hoarse shout, finding his own release. I feel the hot spurts of his seed painting my walls as he pulses inside me. He collapses on top of me, a satisfied groan rumbling through his chest.

For long moments, we simply breathe together, hearts gradually slowing from their frantic gallop.

Eventually, Marcus rolls off me, tucking me against his side. I rest my head on his chest, and it's not long before I feel the rhythmic breathing of him sleeping.

Silently, I slip from the bed. My bare feet make no sound on the cold floor as I creep toward Marcus's office. The door looms before me, a portal to the unknown. My hand trembles as I reach for the handle.

I pause, torn between loyalty and the need to know. Is this betrayal? Or self-preservation? The darkness offers no answers, only the promise of revelations I may not be prepared to face.

Taking a deep breath, I turn the handle and step inside.

The file lies open on his desk, a Pandora's box of secrets. My trembling fingers trace the edges of a photograph—a woman's face, eyes wide with terror. My stomach churns as I read the report beneath.

"No," I whisper, the word a ghostly echo in the silent room. "It can't be."

But there it is, in black and white. Marcus Blackwood, assassin. His enemy's mother, executed with cold precision. My mind reels, unable to reconcile this monstrous act with the man who holds me at night.

I stumble from the office, bile rising in my throat. The walls seem to close in, suffocating me. Marcus stirs, his blue eyes opening to find me standing there, shaking.

"Alana?" His voice is rough with sleep. "What's wrong?"

"How could you?" The words tear from my lips, raw and anguished. "That woman...you killed her."

He sits up slowly, realization dawning on his face. "You went through my files."

"Don't you dare make this about me," I snarl, backing away. "You're a murderer, Marcus. A cold-blooded killer."

His expression hardens, a mask slipping into place. "There are things you don't understand, Alana."

"Then make me understand!" I cry, my voice breaking. "How can I love a man with so much blood on his hands?"

Marcus rises, reaching for me, but I flinch away. His touch, once a comfort, now feels like a brand of shame.

"Tell me why," I plead, tears streaming down my face. "Give me one reason not to walk out that door right now."

The silence stretches between us, a chasm of secrets and lies. I search his face, desperate for a flicker of the man I thought I knew. But all I see is the haunted eyes of a killer, and I wonder if I ever truly knew him at all.

Marcus's jaw clenches, his eyes burning with an intensity that sends a shiver down my spine. "Can you accept the darkness within me, Alana?" he asks, his voice barely above a whisper.

I recoil, my heart pounding. "I don't know," I answer honestly, my voice trembling. "I don't even know who you are anymore."

He takes a step closer, and I fight the urge to retreat. "I am the man you've always known," he says. "But I'm also the boy who watched his mother die."

My breath catches. "What?"

"The man whose mother I killed," Marcus continues, his voice raw with pain, "he murdered my mother first. I was just a child when I found her body."

The revelation hits me like a physical blow. I stumble back, my mind reeling. "Why didn't you tell me?"

"Because I wanted to protect you from this ugliness," he says, reaching for me again. This time, I let him take my hand. "I've carried this burden alone for so long."

I search his face, seeing the guilt and anguish etched into every line. My heart aches for the boy he was, even as I struggle to reconcile it with the man before me.

"I understand if you can't accept me," Marcus murmurs, his grip on my hand tightening. "But know that everything I've done, I've done to survive. To protect those I love. And I'm never letting you go."

I close my eyes, torn between fear and a love that refuses to die. When I open them again, I see Marcus—all of him, light and dark.

"I love you," I confess.

He blinks. "Excuse me?" His voice is so soft I almost don't hear it.

"You heard me," I whisper, stepping closer

until our bodies are almost touching. "I love you, Marcus Blackwood. All of you, even the parts that terrify me."

He stares at me in disbelief, his icy blue eyes wide and searching. "How?" he rasps, voice cracking. "How can you possibly love a monster like me?"

I cup his face in my hands, my thumbs brushing over the sharp planes of his cheek-bones. "You're not a monster," I murmur fiercely. "You're a survivor. A protector. The man who holds my heart in his hands."

Marcus shakes his head, trying to pull away, but I hold fast. "I've done terrible things, Alana. Unforgivable things. You deserve better than me, but bastard that I am, I refuse to let you go. Do you understand that?" He growls as he fists my hair and forces me to look at him. "I would keep you against your will. That's the kind of man I am."

"I don't care," I snap, fire flashing in my eyes. "I choose you, Marcus. I choose to love you, darkness and all."

His breath hitches, and I see it then—the vulnerability he tries so hard to hide. It's there in the slight tremble of his lips, the sheen of unshed tears in his eyes. My heart clenches at the sight.

"I don't deserve your love," he whispers brokenly. "I'll only taint you, ruin you."

I silence him with a searing kiss, pouring every ounce of my love and acceptance into the press of my lips against his. He resists for a moment before surrendering with a groan, his arms coming around me to crush me against his chest.

We break apart, gasping for air. "You could never ruin me," I breathe against his mouth. "Loving you makes me whole."

Something in Marcus seems to shatter at my words. He buries his face in my neck, his shoulders shaking with silent sobs. I hold him tightly, stroking his hair as he clings to me like a drowning man to a life raft.

"I love you," I murmur over and over, a litany of devotion. "I love you, I love you, I love you."

He lifts his head, and the raw emotion in his gaze steals my breath. "Say it again," he pleads.

"I love you, Marcus Blackwood," I declare without hesitation. "You're my everything."

A sob catches in his throat, and then his eyes

darken. "I'm going to fuck you so hard, you'll never forget that you're mine."

Marcus's eyes blaze with feral intensity as he claims my mouth in a bruising kiss. His hands grip my hips possessively, fingers digging into my flesh hard enough to leave marks.

"Mine," he growls against my lips. "You're mine, Alana. My queen. I'd burn the world down for you."

He spins me around and bends me over the desk, his hardness pressing insistently against my backside. I cry out as he enters me in one swift, punishing thrust. He sets a brutal pace, each snap of his hips driving me higher.

"That's it, take my cock," Marcus snarls, fisting a hand in my hair. "You were made for me, this perfect little cunt mine to ruin."

His filthy words ignite something primal inside me. I arch my back, pushing my hips back to meet his thrusts. The lewd smack of skin against skin echoes obscenely in the room.

"Marcus!" I sob, my nails scrabbling against the wooden surface for purchase. The coil in my belly winds tighter with every fierce stroke.

"I'm going to fuck you so full of my seed," he vows darkly. "Mark you inside and out until everyone knows you belong to me. My cum will be dripping out of your well-used slit for days."

The thought of him claiming me so thoroughly sends me careening over the edge. I come with a silent scream, my walls clamping down on him like a vice. He pistons into me through the aftershocks, prolonging my pleasure until it borders on pain.

"That's my good girl," Marcus praises as I go boneless beneath him. "My perfect little cumslut. I'm going to paint this pretty pussy white."

He pulls out abruptly and flips me over. Before I can catch my breath, he's back inside, fucking me into the desk with renewed vigor. His pelvis grinds against my sensitive clit with every thrust, making me see stars.

"Look at me," he commands, blue eyes wild and feverish. "I want to watch your face when I fill this greedy cunt to the brim."

I lock gazes with him, lost in the maelstrom of lust and love reflected back at me. He leans down to capture my mouth again, the kiss sloppy and desperate. I feel him swell inside me, his thrusts becoming erratic.

"Fuck, I'm close," Marcus grunts, breaking

away to mouth at my neck. "Tell me you want it. Beg for my cum."

"Please," I whimper shamelessly, my hips undulating to meet his. "I need it, Marcus. Give me your cum, make me yours. Ruin me for anyone else."

With a roar, he slams home one final time, burying himself to the hilt as he finds his release. His cock jerks and pulses deep inside me, flooding my womb with his hot seed. I keen at the sensation, my inner muscles milking him for every drop.

Marcus collapses on top of me, his weight a comforting blanket. We lay there panting, our sweat-slicked bodies entwined as we come down from the high. He nuzzles into my neck, pressing tender kisses to my racing pulse.

"I don't know that I know how to love, Alan, but what I feel for you is unlike anything I've ever felt for another human being," he murmurs against my skin, the words a reverent prayer.

Tears prick my eyes at his raw confession. I card my fingers through his damp hair, holding him close.

His confession is more than enough for me.

CHAPTER 7

The cloth over my eyes reeks of chloroform. My head pounds as consciousness creeps back. I try to move, but ropes bite into my wrists and ankles. The chair beneath me is cold metal.

"Welcome back, Alana," A man's voice, gravelly and cruel.

My breath catches.

He tsks. "Marcus should have known better. You think he'd know by now there is nowhere he can hide what he cares about. I'll always find it."

"What do you want?" I rasp, throat dry as sandpaper, even as my mind reels. How did I get here? Did he take me in my sleep straight from Marcus's arms?

"He never should have left you alone," the man hisses in my ear. "You would think the fool would know by now all it takes a split second."

I recoil, trying to get away from the voice.

A dark chuckle.

Footsteps circle me. My skin crawls.

The blindfold is ripped away. Harsh light assaults my eyes. As they adjust, I see the mans' scarred face leering down at me. Behind him, a camera on a tripod.

"Smile for Marcus, sweetheart," he sneers.

Before I can react, pain explodes across my jaw. The taste of blood fills my mouth. Through watering eyes, I see the man's fist pull back for another blow.

"That's enough," a voice calls. "We got what we need."

My head lolls. Shadows dance at the edge of my vision. As consciousness fades, one thought burns through the haze of pain:

Marcus will come for me. And god help these men when he does.

———

I don't know how long I've been here. My mind is incoherent. I'm in and out as needles are pressed into my arm, dragging me under before I'm pulled out again with a cold splash of water. Forced to drink but never to eat.

Over and over the cycle continues. For hours? Days?

My eyes are blinking open when the door explodes inward with a deafening crash. Through the haze of pain and fear, I see him— Marcus, a dark avenging angel silhouetted against the light.

Surely, this isn't just a dream? If it is, it's a damn good one.

His eyes meet mine, and in that instant, I see something snap within him.

Those piercing blue eyes…they snap me back to reality, and I sober.

No, not a dream. Can't be.

Gone is the calculated businessman, the measured strategist. This Marcus is primal, feral, a force of nature unleashed.

He lets out a mighty roar, and then he moves like liquid shadow, faster than I've ever seen. The first man falls before I can blink, neck snapped with a sickening crunch. The second crumples, skull caved in by Marcus's fist.

"Marcus," I whisper, voice hoarse.

He doesn't seem to hear me. His face is a mask of cold fury as he tears through the men. Bodies fall like dominoes, bones shattering under the onslaught of his rage.

I've never seen such violence, such raw, unbridled power. It should terrify me, but all I feel is a dark thrill. This destruction, this carnage—it's all for me.

Blood spatters across Marcus's face as he rips out a man's throat. Our eyes lock, and for a moment, I see a flicker of the man I know— vulnerable, searching for approval.

"Don't stop," I breathe, surprised by the venom in my own voice.

A ghost of a smile touches his lips before he turns back to his grim work. I lose count after twenty bodies hit the floor. When it's over, Marcus stands alone amidst the carnage, chest heaving.

There's only one man left alive. The one who punched me. Marcus has him restrained, but right now, he has eyes only for me.

He approaches me slowly, hands trembling as he unties me. "Alana," he murmurs, "I'm sorry, so sorry."

I touch his blood-streaked face. "Don't be. You came for me."

"Always," he whispers, and I see the weight of that promise in his eyes.

The room reeks of copper and fear. Marcus drags the man's limp form before me, tossing him at my feet like a broken doll. My heart races, a savage rhythm pulsing through my veins.

"How would you like him to die, Alana?" Marcus's voice is low, dangerous.

I stare at the man's bruised face, remembering the sting of his fist. The old Alana would recoil, horrified. But she's gone now, consumed by shadows.

"Slowly," I whisper, surprised by the coldness in my voice.

Marcus's eyes gleam with approval. He produces a blade, its edge winking in the dim light. "Show me," he murmurs.

My hand trembles as I take the knife. The man whimpers, eyes wide with terror. I hesitate, teetering on the precipice of no return.

"You don't have to—" Marcus starts, but I silence him with a look.

The first cut is shallow, tentative. The man's scream pierces the air. Something dark unfurls within me, a terrible hunger awakening.

"More," I breathe, passing the knife back to Marcus.

He obliges, his methods more practiced, more cruel. I watch, entranced, as the man's life ebbs away. With each pained gasp, each desperate plea, I feel myself slipping further into the abyss.

When it's over, we stand drenched in red, panting. The air crackles with tension, with unspeakable desire. Marcus pulls me close, his grip bruising.

"My queen," he growls, claiming my mouth in a searing kiss.

We come together in a frenzy, all teeth and nails and desperate need. The blood makes everything slick, primal. I lose myself in the sensations, in the intoxicating darkness of Marcus's embrace.

I'm pulling at Marcus's belt, and he's ripping my clothes from my body. His heavy cock springs free, and I instantly fist it, stroking up and down even as my pussy floods with moisture.

Marcus pins me against the cold stone wall, hands gripping my hips hard enough to bruise. He enters me in one brutal thrust, wrenching a guttural moan from my throat. My nails rake down his back, drawing blood, adding to the macabre painting on our skin.

"You're mine," he snarls into my neck, punctuating each word with a punishing snap of his hips. "Only mine."

"Yes," I gasp, the word dissolving into a keening cry as he hits that perfect spot inside me. "Yours, always yours."

We move together, a tangle of blood-slicked limbs and panting breaths. The stench of death surrounds us, but it only fuels our frenzy. With each powerful stroke, Marcus drives me higher, pushing me to the brink of madness.

"Let go," he commands, his hand snaking between us to circle my aching clit. "Come for me, my queen."

I shatter with a scream, my body convulsing around him as ecstasy rips through me. Marcus follows with a roar, spilling deep inside me, claiming me irrevocably.

We cling to each other in the aftermath, foreheads pressed together, chests heaving. The weight of what we've done, what we've become, hangs heavy in the air.

"There's no going back from this," I whisper, voice raw. "Is there?"

Marcus cups my face, his blue eyes boring

into mine with frightening intensity. "No," he says softly. "But I don't want to go back. I want only to go forward, with you by my side as my queen. We're rule this city together."

I search his gaze, seeing the sincerity, the devotion blazing there. In that moment, I know with bone-deep certainty that I would follow this man into the very depths of hell.

Because I'm his salvation, and he's my ruin, but I'd choose him again, every time.

Want more? Go to www.spicy-romance.com for a free book!

Keep reading for an excerpt from Cruel Master:

Chapter 1

I will not cry.

I will not cry.

Tears begin streaming down my cheeks.

Fuck, I'm crying.

But, damn it, how could I not?

I scream into my gag and writhe, my body flopping back and forth across the floor of the dirty van. The floor feels sticky against my legs, and I don't even want to contemplate what's contributing to that slimy texture. My hands are bound painfully behind my back, and my ankles are tied together too.

It's as cold as an icebox in here, and I'm freezing in my cut-off jean shorts and flimsy little tank top. My nipples pebble painfully, and goosebumps break out on my flesh.

I squeeze my eyes shut and focus on breathing in and out through my nose. It's hard to engage in meditative breathing when panic is making your chest so tight you feel like you're going to have a heart attack even though you're only nineteen years old.

Only nineteen years old. Naïve. Stupid.

I should have known better. My sister and I have loved to binge-watch Lifetime movies ever since we were little girls. I should have seen it coming. It had all the makings of a kidnapping flick written all over it, yet I still took the bait like the desperate little fool I am.

When the photographer in the mall singled me out and told me I'd make a perfect model, I should have seen it coming.

I've seen this very scenario played out in countless movies on LMN, yet I still fell for it.

I believed I was different, that I was untouchable, that nothing so horrible as kidnapping could really happen to me. Is that how the other girls whom this has happened to felt?

I also wanted to believe that I really was pretty enough to be a model, that I could start making some real money and change things for my sister and me. No more working two dead-end jobs, scraping by from paycheck to paycheck. No more going to the local food banks just to make sure my little sister had enough food. I'm not college material, and even if I was, it takes money to go to school. Even if I'd gotten grants or scholarships, it takes money to live, especially when you have a kid sister to take care of.

My heart twists at the thought of Gia. My god, what will she do without me? She's only fifteen, too young to take care of herself, but I know my sister. She'll do everything she can to avoid going back into foster care. It was hell for us both. That's why as soon as I turned eighteen, I did everything I could to prove myself responsible so I could get custody of her.

I promised her we'd never be separated again, and now I'm being ripped from her.

What will she think happened to me? Surely, she'll know I didn't abandon her like our piece-of-shit mother. God, please don't let her end up on the streets. I've fought so hard to keep us both off them. I've seen too many of us foster kids end up there, chewed up and spat out by society. I don't want that for my baby sis.

Fresh tears rush to my eyes at the thought of my baby sis spiraling into a depression, thinking that the responsibility became too much for me and I bailed on her.

I flail again in frustration as sobs overtake me. My scream is muffled against the gag, but I have to let it out anyway.

The guy had sounded so legit. He had a business card and everything and gave me an official time and place to meet him for a test shoot.

As soon as I walked into the decrepit-looking old warehouse, I knew something was wrong. A shiver had run up my spine, and I'd turned to hightail it out of there, but it was already too late.

I felt the prick of the needle against my skin, and this is how I woke up.

Bound and gagged in the back of a dirty old van.

I try to be smart and take note of my surroundings, but it's so dark in here I can hardly make out anything. There's a sliver of light peaking in from the front where the driver sits, but there aren't any windows back here, of course, so I can't try to note any landmarks or street signs.

The light is flashing soft and yellow, though, like it does when you're driving down the street at night.

So, it's night. I don't know yet if that knowledge will help me or how, but I make note of it. It's nighttime. Maybe it will let me get a sense of time if nothing else.

I have to be smart. I think of all those real-life crime shows Gia and I watched together and how the girls who ended up escaping made note of everything they could even if they couldn't see anything.

I try to remember every turn we make and time the minutes between each one. We turned left, then right after about two minutes, then right again after five? Then left again. No, wait, or was it right? And how much time has it been? There are sixty seconds in a minute, and I counted to three hundred fifty since last time...

Fuck this! I scream into my gag again in frustration. I'm not smart enough for this! I don't have a good enough memory for numbers on the best of days—much less when I'm bound and gagged like a critter soon to be roasted over a pit.

I lay there crying and breathing heavily as fear sluices through my veins. What's going to happen to me? Is he going to kill me? Rape me? Is he going to torture me?

I begin to shake uncontrollably when I remember all the crime documentaries I've seen and some of the horrible ways the people in them died.

Is this guy a serial killer? Is there any way I can reason with him when we eventually get to wherever he's taking me? Try to humanize yourself to the predator. That's what they always say on those shows.

I have to try to make him like me, try not to show my fear because if it's fear he gets off on, then that's only going to amp him up.

Or, it might just piss him off if I don't react the way he wants me to.

More tears stream down my face at the helplessness of my situation. I don't know what to do. It's a gamble either way.

I close my eyes and think of Gia. I go through every good memory of my sister I have. Us playing together in the park. Her tenth birthday when I stole us both a pair of skates and snuck us into the skating rink. The day I officially adopted her.

Memories of my sister calm me as I remind myself that I have a reason to fight. I have my sister.

I begin trying to pay attention to any little details I can again. I'm not being jostled around as much anymore, so we're on a smoother road. A highway maybe? What kind of road were we on before then?

My heart begins hammering against my ribcage when my body sways forward as the brakes engage.

We're slowing down, coming to a stop.

Surely, we're not on a highway then. Probably a private drive then? A paved one?

The engine dies, and then I hear the slam of the door as someone gets out of the front. It sounded like it came from the passenger side, though—not the driver's side.

My stomach lurches. Does that mean there are two of them? One I have yet to see?

Oh god, being tortured and raped and killed by one monster is bad enough, but two?

Please don't let me be that unlucky, I pray to any deity out there that will listen.

The door opens, and I blink against the sudden, blinding light of a cell phone's flash-light shining right in my face.

"Alright, girl. Up we go," a voice I recognize as the photographer's from the mall speaks coldly.

He moves the flashlight up, and I look up at his goatee and bald head. He's big and muscular with a plain white T-shirt and low-slung jeans. Not exactly handsome but not hideous either. I'd thought he looked artistic back at the mall. He'd looked like a legitimate photographer in my mind, but now I see him for what he is.

A criminal.

He reaches in to grab me by the arms and haul me up, but when I see his big hands looming toward me, I forget everything I'd told myself I was going to do.

I act on pure instinct instead and twist onto my back until my feet are up in the air. The weight of my spine on my hands makes my wrists ache, but I ignore it.

I lift my bound feet and kick as hard as I can straight at the man's face.

Get Cruel Master here: Cruel Master.